D1513729

Illustrated by Vince Reid

First Published
May 08 in Great Britain by

PUBLISHING

© Adam Bushnell 2008

The moral right of the author has been asserted in accordance with the
Copyright, Designs and Patents Act 1988

ISBN-10: 1-905637-50-0
ISBN-13: 978-1-905637-50-8

Educational Printing Services Limited
Albion Mill, Water Street, Great Harwood, Blackburn BB6 7QR
Telephone: (01254) 882080                    Fax: (01254) 882010
E-mail: enquiries@eprint.co.uk              Website: www.eprint.co.uk

# Contents

'For my family, for my friends'

# 1: Anansi and the Sheep
## (Caribbean)

Anansi was sometimes a spider and sometimes a man . . . and this made him a sort of Spiderman! He could shoot out web lines, climb walls and even had a spider sense!

✻✻✻✻

One evening Anansi was walking past a farm when he saw a really miserable looking sheep standing in a field surrounded by a tall wooden fence.

1

"What's the matter with you Sheep?" asked Anansi.

"Oh, Anansi!" cried Sheep, "I'm so miserable. The farmer who is supposed to look after me doesn't look after me at all. He never feeds me; all I have to eat is this brown, dried up bit of grass. He never gives me anything to drink; all I have to drink is this muddy puddle. I'm so miserable."

Anansi felt so sorry for Sheep that he used his web lines to lift him over the fence.

Then Anansi and Sheep ran away as fast as they could;
RUN! RUN! RUN! RUN! RUN!

Until eventually the sun started to rise in the sky; it was morning. With a bang

Anansi and Sheep ran straight into a tiger.

"AHA!" roared the tiger. "A spider and a sheep! That's exactly what I want for my breakfast!"

And the tiger began to crouch, ready to jump on Anansi and Sheep.

But Anansi said, "No wait! Don't jump on us, don't eat us . . . erm . . . because the sky is falling, that's why we are running as fast as we can. You'd better run away too before it falls on your head!"

"AAAARGGH!" screamed the tiger and ran off.

Then Anansi and Sheep ran away as fast as they could again;
RUN! RUN! RUN! RUN! RUN!

But with a boom Anansi and the sheep ran straight into a lion.

"AHA!" growled the lion. "A spider and a sheep! That's exactly what I want for my breakfast!"

And the lion began to crouch, ready to pounce on Anansi and Sheep.

But Anansi said, "No wait! Don't jump on us, don't eat us . . . because the sky is falling, that's why we are running as fast as we can. You'd better run away too before it falls on your head!"

"AAAARGGH!" screamed the lion and he ran off too.

Then Anansi and Sheep ran away as fast as they could yet again;
RUN! RUN! RUN! RUN! RUN!

But with a bash Anansi and the sheep ran straight into a hyena.

"AHA!" laughed the hyena. "A spider and a sheep! That's exactly what I want for my breakfast!"

And the hyena began to crouch, ready to leap on Anansi and Sheep.

But Anansi said, "No wait! Don't jump on us, don't eat us because the sky is falling, that's why we are running as fast as we can. You'd better run away too before it falls on your head!"

"AAAARGGH!" screamed the hyena and ran off.

Then Anansi and Sheep ran away as fast as they could once more;
RUN! RUN! RUN! RUN! RUN!

Until eventually they came across a field filled with luscious green grass. They ran into the field and Sheep started to eat the grass as fast as he could.
MUNCH! MUNCH! MUNCH! MUNCH!

Just then Sheep noticed a crystal clear

lake nearby, so they ran over to the lake and Sheep started to drink the water as fast as he could.

SLURP! SLURP! SLURP! SLURP! SLURP!

When Sheep had finished drinking he noticed it was getting dark and said to Anansi, "Do you think we can sleep up in that tree over there tonight, just so that we know that this field is safe?"

Anansi used his web lines to make a hammock, then they both climbed up into the hammock and were just nodding off to sleep when along came the tiger, the lion and the hyena. They sat underneath the tree and began talking to each other.

"Did you know," roared the tiger, "that I had a silly trick played on me today by a spider and a sheep. They told me some ridiculous story about the sky falling on my head and I must admit it; I did believe them."

"Do you know," growled the lion, "the same thing happened to me."

"HA! HA!" laughed the hyena. "The same thing happened to me too!"

"If I ever meet those two again," roared the tiger, "I'm going to bite their heads off."

"And I'm going to bite their legs off," growled the lion.

"And I'll crunch their bones to dust," laughed the hyena.

Now Anansi and Sheep heard every word of this up in the tree and Anansi whispered to Sheep, "SHHHHHHHHH! Be really quiet, otherwise they'll hear us."

"B – B - But I need the toilet!" said Sheep.

"You what!?" spluttered Anansi.

"I – I – I need the toilet, I had too much to drink down at the lake and now I've got to wee!"

"You can't go to the toilet now!" answered Anansi. "They'll eat us up!"

"It's no good," said Sheep, "I really need to go!"

Then Sheep wriggled and squirmed so

much that he fell out of the hammock and
with a BANG! landed right on top of the
tiger, the lion and the hyena!

"AAAAARRRGGGGHHHH!!!" they screamed. "The sky is falling! The sky is falling!" as they ran off never to be seen again.

Well Sheep got to live in that luscious, green field. He got to eat the grass as often as he wanted to. He got to drink from the lake as often as he wanted to. But, best of all, he got to go to the toilet whenever he wanted to.

# 2: The One Hundred Children

## (Romania)

There once lived a farmer and his wife. They loved each other, their animals and their farm, but their hearts were filled with sadness; this was because they had no children.

One day while the farmer was working in the field, his wife Mary was feeding the sheep when she met a very old man sitting at the roadside.

"Good day to you, sir," she said

cheerfully. "How are you today? You look hungry; perhaps you would like to share my lunch with me?"

As she said these words she pulled a knotted handkerchief from her backpack, opened it up and offered some bread and cheese to the old man.

The old man smiled and said, "I may look old and frail to you, but I'm as fit as a fiddle. But you . . . you look very sad. Tell me, what's the matter?"

"Me?" replied Mary, "I'm happy enough. I have a good husband and the farm keeps us comfortable."

"Yet there is sadness behind your eyes," continued the old man. "Tell me. What troubles you? Perhaps I can help."

"I don't think you can help me," smiled Mary, "for what I wish for is children."

"Children?" laughed the old man. "Is that all?"

"Oh yes," replied Mary, "just children."

And with that, the old man leapt up into the air, shook his stick at the clouds while laughing and muttered a silent prayer. He then limped off up the road chuckling away to himself.

Mary walked home after she had finished her jobs and she could not believe her eyes. There, running in and out of the house were children . . . many children!

Her husband was laughing and playing with them all.

"Mary! Mary!" he called, "Look! We have children! Lots of children!"

Mary hugged her husband tightly and wondered as to where all of these children had come from. They watched as the children played in the garden, ran around the house, climbed in and out of the windows.

At supper time, Mary fed them all, her husband bathed them all and then they both tucked them all up safe and snug in blankets all over the house.

When every child was sleeping they counted them all up.

"One hundred children!" gasped Mary. "How on earth will we feed and clothe this many?"

"It'll be alright," said her husband and he collapsed asleep in his armchair fast asleep.

But Mary couldn't sleep. She was worried.

She fretted and wrung her hands until at last she packed a backpack with a blanket and some food then woke her husband.

"It's no good," said Mary, "we'll never be able to look after this many children with what we can provide on the farm. I'm off to seek our fortune."

"Alright then," yawned her husband, "have fun."

With that he went back to sleep.

Mary walked all night long until at sunrise she found a herd of sheep loose on a mountainside and their shepherd cowering behind a large rock.

"Whatever is the matter?" asked Mary. "Surely you're not afraid of sheep!"

"I – I – It's not the sheep I'm scared of!" the shepherd stammered back. "I . . . It's a giant! He comes here every sunrise and feeds on my sheep!"

Suddenly there was a boom!

BOOM!

BOOM!

BOOM!

BOOM!

Getting louder and louder and louder still. The giant stomped over the top of the mountain and grabbed two sheep in each of its massive hands.

"Hey you!" shouted Mary. "Stop that!"

The giant was so surprised that he dropped the two sheep and plodded warily over to Mary.

"WHO ARE YOU?" he thundered.

"My name is Mary the Strong," shouted Mary bravely.

"HOW STRONG ARE YOU?" asked the giant.

"I'm so strong that I can squeeze the blood out of a stone!" Mary said confidently.

"OH YEAH?" boomed the giant. "SHOW ME!"

Mary dropped her backpack to the ground. With one hand she reached inside and grabbed some red berries she had packed for her lunch and with the other she picked up a stone.

Now in the dim light of sunrise the giant could only see the large stone in Mary's hands, so when she squeezed the stone and crushed the berries onto it, all the giant saw was Mary squeezing blood out of a stone.

"BLIMEY!" he roared, "THAT'S AMAZING! I CAN'T EVEN DO THAT! YOU

SHOULD COME BACK TO MY CAVE. MY MOTHER AND I ARE ALWAYS LOOKING FOR STRONG SLAVES – ERM – I MEAN FRIENDS TO HELP US WITH OUR WORK."

Mary thought for a few moments. She knew that giants often had great stashes of treasure in their caves, so she smiled and said, "I'd be glad to!"

The giant picked Mary up with its massive hands and stomped off across the mountain and way off across the countryside.

Eventually after walking for a whole day they came to a large cave just as the sun was setting. The giant set Mary down as they both stepped inside.

The giant's mother saw them entering. She was even bigger than the giant! But

Mary gave a brave and loud, "Hello!"

"WHO'S THIS THEN?" the giant's mother screeched at her son.

"SHE'S THE STRONGEST WOMAN I'VE EVER MET. SHE'S EVEN STRONGER THAN ME! I'VE BROUGHT HER BACK HERE TO BE OUR SLAVE – ERM – I MEAN FRIEND."

The giant's mother looked terrified and said to Mary, "YOU MUST BE EXHAUSTED AFTER ALL YOUR TRAVELLING. HERE  - YOU CAN SLEEP IN THIS BED TONIGHT."

Mary was shown a gigantic bed and had difficulty climbing into it. But when she did the giant's mother grabbed her son's arm and dragged him outside.

"WHAT ARE YOU DOING BRINGING

HER BACK HERE?" she whispered. "IF
SHE'S SO STRONG SHE MIGHT STEAL
OUR GOLD. WHEN SHE'S ASLEEP WE'LL
BEAT HER TO DEATH WITH OUR BIG
STICKS!"

Now the problem with giants is that
they aren't very good at whispering so Mary
heard every word. She leapt from her bed
and grabbed several large rocks from the
floor. She then put them in the gigantic bed,
covered them with the blanket and hid
underneath the bed.

In the middle of the night Mary peered
out from under the bed and saw the giant
and his mother creeping up holding two
sticks as big as trees.

They then bashed and bashed and
bashed at the bed and went back to their
own beds chuckling away.

Once they had gone, Mary leapt up into the gigantic bed and pushed the rocks over the side.

In the morning the giant and his mother were sitting down in their cave to a breakfast of a herd of cows when Mary interrupted them.

"Morning!" she called cheerfully.

"AAAGGHHH!" the giant and his mother screamed. "WHAT ARE YOU DOING HERE? DIDN'T YOU FEEL ANYTHING IN THE NIGHT?"

"Oh, I did feel moths tickling my body, but that was all," she replied.

"AAAGGHHH!" the giant and his mother screamed again.

"SHE REALLY IS STRONG! HOW WILL WE EVER GET RID OF HER?" said the giant to his mother.

"ERM, LISTEN MARY THE STRONG," the giant's mother said cautiously, "IF WE GIVE YOU A POT OF GOLD WILL YOU LEAVE US ALONE AND NEVER COME BACK?"

"Hmm," Mary said thoughtfully, "I'll tell you what. You give me a pot of gold and if your son promises to leave that shepherd alone, then you've got a deal."

"DONE!" the giant's mother said quickly, "NOW GO GIVE HER A LIFT HOME!"

The giant's mother gave Mary a pot of gold which she stuffed into her backpack and the giant lifted her up once more into its massive hand.

Then they were off again across the countryside until at last they came to the

mountain where the shepherd and his sheep
lived. The shepherd was cowering behind
that same rock when he heard the giant
coming, but was soon very relieved when
Mary made the giant promise that he would
never bother the shepherd again.

After walking only a few giant steps
they were back at Mary's farm. There her
husband and her hundred children saw her
coming, being carried by the giant. The
children screamed excitedly then ran as
fast as they could towards Mary and the
giant.

"WHO ARE ALL THOSE CHILDREN?"
asked the giant.

"Those are my children, you can put me
down here," answered Mary, "and they are
so excited because I promised them giant

stew for their dinner."

"AAAGGHHH!" screeched the terrified giant and he stomped off as fast as his legs would carry him.

Mary showed her husband and their hundred children the gold and they all lived happy lives together on that farm.

# 3: The Monster Medusa
## (Greek)

Perseus was a brave and handsome hero who lived with his very beautiful mother. He lived in a land that was ruled by a grumpy king.

One day the grumpy king sent for Perseus's mother and said, "Will you marry me?"

"NO!" answered Perseus's mother and ran back home as fast as she could.

The next day the grumpy king sent for

Perseus's mother again and said, "Will you marry me?"

"NO!" answered Perseus's mother and ran back home as fast as she could.

The same thing happened the next day.

And the day after that.

And the day after that.

Until Perseus decided he had had enough. He walked into the grumpy king's palace and said, "Leave my mother alone!"

The grumpy king stared at Perseus for a while with a frown on his face. But then he smiled and said, "I will leave your mother alone . . . IF . . . you bring me the head of the monster Medusa!"

Everyone in the palace gasped because nobody could do that. Medusa was a monster so ugly that she had snakes for hair, so ugly that she had green warts covering her scaly body, so ugly that if she was to look at you even once she would turn you to stone.

But Perseus said, "I'll do it!" and everyone in the palace laughed and laughed and laughed.

Perseus was no fool. He knew that he would need some help to defeat the monster Medusa. So he walked and walked and walked until he came to the house of a wise, old man.

Perseus knocked at the door and the wise, old man opened it. He had no teeth and no hair but smiled as he said, "'Ello! Who are you?"

"My name is Perseus and I need to know how to kill the monster Medusa!"

"You big fool!" said the wise, old man. "Nobody can do that. Medusa is a monster so ugly that she has snakes for hair, so ugly that she has green warts covering her scaly body, so ugly that if she was to look at you even once, she would turn you to stone. You big fool!"

But Perseus explained everything to the wise, old man. He told him all about his mother and the grumpy king.

Finally the wise, old man said, "Go and see the three witches who live in the cave by the sea. They'll tell you how to kill the monster Medusa."

Perseus thanked the old man and set off again. He walked and walked and walked until he came to the cave of the three witches.

Perseus peered into the cave and saw that the three witches only had one eyeball between them and they were fighting over the eyeball like this . . .

"It's my turn with the eyeball!" one would screech.

"No it's not, you had it yesterday!" another would squeal.

"Yes, you did, you always have it! It's my turn!" the third would scream.

On and on they went until at last they dropped the eyeball onto the floor. Perseus rushed in, grabbed the eyeball and ran back to the entrance of the cave.

"I have your eyeball and you can't have it back until you tell me how to kill the monster Medusa!"

The three witches gave Perseus a helmet to make him invisible, some boots to make him fly, a shiny shield so that he didn't have to look at the monster Medusa and a sharp sword to chop off her head.

Perseus thanked the witches, gave them back their eyeball and shouted to his boots, "TAKE ME TO MEDUSA!"

Suddenly Perseus flew up into the air, higher and higher and higher he went. Until at last he arrived at Medusa's palace.

He put on his helmet to make him invisible and used his shiny shield like a mirror to look around the palace.

He crept past many stone statues until he finally found Medusa, reflected in his mirror, sleeping on the floor.

Now even though Perseus was invisible, the snakes in Medusa's hair knew that someone was there and hissed loudly . . .

HHHHHHHSSSSSSSSSSSSSS!!!!!

So loudly that they woke Medusa up!

Medusa took the bow and her arrows from her back and began shooting them all over the palace.

Perseus had to duck and jump, duck and jump, duck and jump, until he reached Medusa.

Then he drew his sharp sword and with a mighty CHOP! off came Medusa's head.

Perseus put the head into a sack, took off the helmet and shouted to his boots, "TAKE ME HOME!"

Instantly Perseus flew up into the air, higher and higher and higher he went. Until at last he arrived at the grumpy king's palace.

Perseus walked into the palace and saw his beautiful mother standing next to the king.

The grumpy king said, "Have you done it then? Have you brought me the head of the monster Medusa?"

"Yes I have!" Perseus said bravely.

Everyone in the palace laughed and laughed and laughed.

Perseus then shouted, "All those who love me . . . look at the floor!"

Perseus's mother looked at the floor, his friends and his family looked at the floor and Perseus took the head of the monster Medusa out of the sack. He showed it all around the palace.

All those people who weren't looking at the floor were instantly turned to stone . . . even the grumpy king!

Perseus then took the head down to the beach and threw it into the sea where it could not do any more harm.

Then Perseus and his mother both went home where they lived happily for the rest of their days.

# 4: The Sockburn Worm
## (England)

In the land of Sockburn, at the very southern point of County Durham, Lord Conyers was riding on his horse. He was surveying his land that was filled with happy and hard working families.

He stopped at a hillside and smiled.

But this smile was soon gone.

For there was suddenly a great rumbling noise from below the ground; a noise that made the earth shake and tremble. Lord Conyers held his reigns tightly but he was soon knocked off his horse.

And from deep under the ground emerged a dragons head, then a long, scaly neck. The dragon oozed and slimed its way from its underground home and slowly uncoiled itself.

Lord Conyers let out a scream as he looked at the hideous monster. It was a worm! A dragon with no legs! Lord Conyers had heard of these creatures living in Lambton and Bamburgh and he knew of their appetite!

He leapt back onto his horse and sped away, but the worm was too quick. It roared a terrible roar . . .
    ROOOOAAAARRRR!
and gave chase.

It soon caught up with Lord Conyers and it let out a terrible gas . . .
    PHWPPPPPPPPPPPPPPPPT!

And Lord Conyers collapsed onto the ground choking to death.

Then the worm oozed and slimed its way across the countryside devouring ducks, chewing chickens, killing cows and gulping goats.

When it was satisfied the worm disappeared back underground with another great rumbling noise.

Lord Conyers' son, Sir John Conyers, was out hunting when he heard the commotion. Sir John rode as swiftly as the wind until he came to the place where his own father lay dead on the floor.

He wept great tears of sorrow but these tears were soon replaced by tears of anger. He knew that the only thing that could have caused such devastation was a worm.

So Sir John called together a team of brave and fearless knights. Knights wearing shining armour, knights carrying swords and shields.

Together Sir John and the knights rode across the countryside searching for the worm.

And they did not have to search for long. For again there was that great rumbling noise coming from underground. Then the worm emerged and oozed and slimed its way at great speed towards the knights.

Sir John sounded a bugle and the knights charged at the worm.

The worm roared its terrible roar . . .

ROOOOAAAARRRR!

and when the knights were close enough it let out its terrible gas . . .

PHWPPPPPPPPPPPPPPPPT!

And all of the knights collapsed onto the ground choking to death.

Sir John, realising he needed another plan, rode off as quickly as he could. As he did he heard the great rumbling noise of the worm disappearing back underground.

Eventually Sir John came to the house of a local wise woman. He climbed down from his horse and knocked at the door.

"Who is it, dear?" cackled the wise woman.

"It's me, Sir John Conyers. Please can I come in and talk with you?"

"Come in, dear," she said.

Sir John stepped inside the wise woman's house and sat next to her by the fire. He explained everything about the worm, his father and the knights.

The wise woman stood up and stirred her cauldron sitting above the fire three times, then she said the magic words, which were . . . "Wuggy! Wuggy! Wuggy!" clapped her hands three times and said, "Chop! Chop! Chop!"

There was a FLASH and a BANG!

Then there, rising out of the cauldron, was a long, double handed, broadsword.

"This sword is called the Falchion, dear," she said, "with this you will slay the worm, dear,"

Then she stirred her cauldron again three times, then she said the magic words, "Wuggy! Wuggy! Wuggy!" clapped her hands three times and said, "Phwpt! Phwpt! Phwpt!"

There was another FLASH and another BANG!

Then there, rising out of the cauldron, was something that Sir John had never seen before.

"What's that?" he asked.

"It's scuba diving gear, dear," she answered. "It's from the future, dear. With this you won't be able to breathe in the worm's terrible gases, dear."

Sir John pulled the wetsuit over his armour, pulled the flippers over his boots, strapped the oxygen tank to his back, put in his breathing regulator and strapped the mask over his helmet.

Then, taking the Falchion in one hand, he thanked the wise woman and climbed back onto his horse.

He hadn't been riding long when there came that loud rumbling noise from underground.

Sir John held the reigns in one hand and the Falchion in the other like a lance.

The worm oozed and slimed its way towards him, then it roared its terrible roar . . . ROOOOAAAARRRR!
and when it was close enough to Sir John it let out its terrible gas . . .

PHWPPPPPPPPPPPPPPPPT!

But with the scuba diving gear on Sir John was completely unharmed.

The worm roared with fury . . .

ROOOOAAAARRRR!

and let out more and more terrible gases . . .

PHWPPPPPPPPPPPPPPPPPT!

PHWPPPPPPPPPPPPPPPPPT!

PHWPPPPPPPPPPPPPPPPPT!

PHWPPPPPPPPPPPPPPPPPT!

PHWPPPPPPPPPPPPPPPPPT!

Sir John charged forward and pierced the worm's heart with the Falchion.

The worm slumped onto the ground dead, then fizzed and sizzled into the earth until there was nothing left.

Sir John quickly became a local hero and was made the new lord of the land.

Whenever a new lord was proclaimed the Falchion was passed on generation to generation.

And if you don't believe this story, you can still see the Falchion today hanging up in Durham Cathedral.

# 5: How the Hyena got his Laugh
## (African)

A long, long, long, long, long, long, long, time ago, there lived a hyena in Africa. That long ago Hyena behaved very differently from the way he does today because instead of laughing all of the time, he was really, REALLY grumpy.

Hyena would sit around all day long making everyone else around him feel just as miserable.

One day, along slithered Snake who

hissed with a . . .

HSSSSSSSSSSSSSSSSSSSSSS!
HSSSSSSSSSSSSSSSSSSSSSS!

"Hyena," she hissed, "would you like to hear a joke? It might cheer you up!"

"Slither off, Snake," said Hyena grumpily.

But Snake ignored him and said, "What subjects are snakes good at in school?"

"Dunno," answered Hyena while looking in the other direction.

"Hiss-tory!" laughed Snake.

"That's not funny!" shrugged Hyena and Snake slithered off.

The next day, along swung Monkey who

laughed with a . . .

OO – OO – AA – AA!

"Hyena," he laughed, "would you like to hear a joke? It might cheer you up!"

"Swing off, Monkey," said Hyena grumpily.

But Monkey ignored him and said, "How do monkeys make toast?"

"Dunno," answered Hyena while looking in the other direction.

"They put it under the gorilla!" laughed Monkey.

"That's not funny!" shrugged Hyena and Monkey began swinging back to the trees.

The day after that, along stomped Elephant who snorted with a . . .
PPPRRRRRRRRRRRRRPPPPPPPPPPP!

"Hyena," he snorted, "would you like to hear a joke? It might cheer you up!"

"Snort off, Elephant," said Hyena grumpily.

But Elephant ignored him and said, "What's more difficult than getting an elephant in the back of a car?"

"Dunno," answered Hyena while looking

in the other direction.

"Getting TWO elephants in the back of a car!" laughed Elephant.

"That's not funny!" shrugged Hyena and Elephant stomped off.

The animals had decided that they were sick of Hyena's bad attitude. He made them all feel so grumpy that they went to the beach.

There Snake, Monkey and Elephant went to see the funniest animal of them all . . . Clown Fish.

They called out across the sea, "Clown Fish! Clown Fish! We need you!"

Clown Fish leapt out of the water and

into a rock pool nearby.

"Wa-hey!" laughed the clown fish. "What can I do for you three!"

The animals looked at each other and Snake hissed, "We need to cheer up Hyena. He's sssssssoooooo grumpy!"

"We thought you could help!" laughed Monkey.

"We need you to tell us a joke that will definitely make Hyena laugh," snorted Elephant.

Clown Fish looked at the three animals and then smiled a big smile. "I've got just the thing!" chuckled Clown Fish as he told the animals the perfect joke for Hyena.

The animals rushed back to Hyena after thanking Clown Fish.

"Hyena!" all the animals shouted. "Would you like to hear another joke? It will definitely cheer you up!"

Hyena just shrugged grumpily.

The animals all said together, "A lion is walking along in the jungle. He goes up to a snake and says, 'Roar! Who's the king of the jungle?' The snake says, 'You are, lion.' The lion goes up to a monkey and says, 'Roar! Who's the king of the jungle?' The monkey says, 'You are, lion.'

The lion goes up to an elephant and says, 'Roar! Who's the king of the jungle?' The elephant smacks him with his trunk, picks him up, twirls him around over his head a few times, smashes him into a tree, and tosses him about thirty feet. The lion gets up and says, "Blimey! You don't have to get so annoyed, just because you don't know the answer."

Hyena looked at the three animals. Then his face began to twitch. Then all of a sudden Hyena went, "BWA! HA! HA! HA! HA! HA! HA! That's the funniest joke I've ever heard! HA! HA! HA! HA! HA! HA!

HAAAAAAAAAAAAA!!!"

From that day Hyena never stopped laughing. And that is how the Hyena got his laugh, all thanks to the little Clown Fish.

# 6: The Rich Lord's Wife
## (Norway)

Once there lived a rich Lord who lived in a huge castle. He owned many acres of land, wore fine clothes, had money in the bank, a Playstation 3, you name it – he had it.

But he was lonely. For although he had a great many possessions, he had no wife.

One day he was out riding on his fine stallion when he passed a poor farmer's house. Now this farmer lived on the Lord's land, so the Lord thought nothing at all of simply riding his horse through the poor farmer's back garden to look at the many flowers that bloomed there.

As the rich Lord did so, he noticed the poor farmer's daughter cutting some flowers and placing them in a basket. She was young and she was beautiful.

He brought his horse along side her and said, "Good day to you my pretty. I was just wondering, perhaps you would consider becoming my wife?"

He flashed a dazzling smile and winked at her as he said this.

"What?!" she spluttered. "I'm not going to marry you. You're old . . . and you're ugly. No way!"

And with that she stomped off into the house.

The rich Lord was in a terrible temper. Nobody had ever said no to him before! He rode his horse round to the front of the poor farmer's house, slid down from his saddle and hammered at the door.

"Erm, yes, my lord? Can I help you?" asked the poor farmer as he answered the door.

"Indeed you can!" boomed the rich Lord. "I just asked your daughter to marry me . . .

and she said no! Is it not a great honour for me to propose to your daughter?"

"Indeed it is sir," replied the poor farmer.

"And would she not be rich beyond her wildest dreams?" demanded the rich Lord.

"Indeed she would sir," answered the poor farmer.

"And is it not right that she should agree to marry me then, eh?" enquired the rich Lord menacingly.

"Erm, well I suppose it is sir."

"Right then!" bellowed the rich Lord. "You have just promised me your daughter's hand in marriage!"

"But . . . ," began the poor farmer.

"No 'buts' man! A promise is a promise," said the rich Lord shaking his hands in the air and walking back to his stallion. "I will set the wedding for one week's time at the church. And your daughter had better be there!"

With that the rich Lord steered his horse away and sped off to his castle.

A week later and the wedding was prepared. The church was decorated with flowers from top to bottom. The reception would take place in the field next to the church where a gigantic marquee stood. The tables sagged under the weight of the food and the drink. People were dressed in their finest clothes. Everyone in the land had turned up to witness the marriage and join in the celebration . . . everyone that is except for the poor farmer's daughter!

The rich Lord grew more and more impatient as he stood waiting inside the church.

At last, he clapped his hands and sent for his messenger.

"Messenger!" he bellowed. "Go to the poor farmer's house and demand what I have been promised!"

"Right away sir!" replied the messenger and he sped off as fast as his feet could carry him.

When he arrived at the poor farmer's house, breathless and panting he knocked at the door.

The poor farmer's daughter answered the door and said, "Yes? Can I help you?"

"Right," said the messenger, "the rich Lord says that he wants what's been promised to him."

"Oh, I see," replied the poor farmer's daughter thinking quickly, "he's talking about a horse! There's a female horse he's been wanting from us. You know - a mare for his stallion. She's down round the back of the garden, help yourself!"

With that the messenger went around the back of the garden, untied the horse and led her to the church as fast as he could. He then tethered her to a tree and rushed to tell the rich Lord he had been successful.

"I've done it!" the messenger said. "She's outside."

"Right then," beamed the rich Lord, "take her to my castle and lead her into my mother's bedroom."

"WHAT?!" gasped the messenger.

"You heard me, now do it," answered the rich Lord gruffly.

"What if she struggles when I'm getting her up the stairs?" asked the messenger rather bemused.

"Then get some friends to help you – now go!" demanded the rich Lord.

So the messenger untied the horse and led her to the rich Lord's castle. With some help he got the horse up the stairs and into the bedroom. He then rushed back to the church and said, "I've done it! She's in your mother's bedroom."

"Excellent," grinned the rich Lord, "now dress her in fine silks and exquisite velvet."

"WHAT??!!" spluttered the messenger.

"You heard me, now do it!"

"OK then," said the messenger as again he sped back to the castle. He then dressed the horse in the finest gown he had ever seen and rushed back to the church.

"I've done it, she's wearing a fine gown!" the messenger said.

"Marvellous," beamed the rich Lord, "now give her some jewellery and some makeup."

"W - WHAT!!!???" stammered the messenger.

"You heard me now do it!"

"OK then," the messenger replied as he sped back to the castle. When he got there he put some lipstick and some eyeliner on the horse. Then he put on some earrings and a necklace. Then at last he rushed back to the church.

"I've done it, she's all made up!" the

messenger said.

"Superb," leered the rich Lord, "now bring her to me . . . I wish to marry her!"

"W – W - WHAT!!!???" gabbled the messenger.

"You heard me now do it!"

"OK then," shrugged the messenger as he sped back to the castle. He then led the horse down the stairs, out of the doors and along the road to the church.

When the messenger got there he flung open the church doors and the whole of the congregation saw the horse in the wedding dress.

They all laughed and laughed and

laughed.

The horse stared at the rich Lord.

The rich Lord stared at the horse.

\*    The horse saw how old and ugly the rich
Lord was and neighed loudly then bolted
from the church as fast as she could.

NEIGGGGGHHHHH!!!

Outside of the church, the rich Lord's stallion saw the horse in the wedding dress and fell in love instantly. The stallion and the mare lived happily ever after.

As for the rich Lord?

That grumpy old miser never did find love or happiness.

*    This story ending was provided by Georgia Lines, aged 4, from the Reception Class, at South Pelaw Infant School, Hilda Park, Chester-le-Street, Co. Durham.

# 7: The Skinny Thief
## (Dutch)

In the town of Sterkdam, in Holland, there was once a thief called Tyl. Tyl was such an amazing thief that he could steal the fork from your hand when you were eating your dinner. Such an incredible thief that he could steal the shoes from your feet and you wouldn't notice he was there!

One cold and miserable winter, Spain declared war on Holland. The Spanish army had destroyed every town and every village across the whole of Holland except for Sterkdam.

Sterkdam was surrounded by huge stone walls that protected the town. The Spanish army had six canons delivered and made a circle of canons around the town walls.

But the Spanish general said, "No! We'll not waste our canon balls on these walls. We have food delivered to us every day, but these people have nothing left. Let them starve inside the walls they hide behind!"

And so everyone inside the walls of Sterkdam went hungry. Waiting and wishing for the Hollanders army to reform and save them from the Spanish.

Nobody was more hungry than Tyl. He decided that the best place to get food would be in prison. Everyone knows that you get three square meals a day in prison.

Tyl allowed himself to be caught and was locked up in the highest cell of Sterkdam prison.

But Tyl had got it wrong. The prisoners had even less food than everyone else!

Tyl became so skinny that he was able to slip through the metal bars on his window. He sat on his window ledge shivering and looked over the town walls at the Spanish army feasting on all of their food.

Then Tyl smiled. He had an idea. He slipped back into his cell and tied all of the sheets from the beds together into a long, white rope. He tied one end to the bars on his window and lowered the rope of sheets onto the snow covered ground below.

Then Tyl slipped back through the bars and climbed down onto the ground. He untied the bottom sheet and pulled it over his head. Now with a white sheet over Tyl's head against the snow covered ground Tyl looked invisible! It was like he was wearing an invisibility cloak!

Tyl sneaked his way through Sterkdam. Sneaked his way to the town walls, sneaked his way through the gates and sneaked up to where the Spanish army were camped. Tyl looked at the canons surrounding the town and smiled to himself.

Then he sneaked up to the tent where the Spanish army kept all of their food, he took out his penknife and made a cut in the tent.

Tyl stole as much as he could carry and hid the food under the white sheet. He stole whole chickens, sides of beef, wheels of cheese, loaves of bread, strings of sausages and sacks of potatoes.

Next, Tyl sneaked his way up to one of the canons and stuffed it full of chickens.

Then up to another and stuffed it full of beef. He stuffed another full of cheese.

Another full of bread. Another with sausages. And another with potatoes. He had stuffed all six canons with the food!

Then Tyl sneaked his way back to the town walls, pulled off his sheet, turned round to the Spanish army and blew the biggest raspberry you have ever heard!

BBBBLLLLLLTTTTHHHH!!!!!!!!!!!!!!!!!!

The Spanish army were furious!

But so were the people of Sterkdam. They pulled Tyl back inside the town and said, "What are you doing you fool! They'll light the canons now for sure!"

Suddenly there was a huge BOOM! and over the walls of the town came whole chickens.

Then BOOM! sides of beef.
BOOM! wheels of cheese.
BOOM! loaves of bread.
BOOM! strings of sausages.
BOOM! sacks of potatoes.

All of the food came raining down on the town of Sterkdam.

Just then the Hollanders army arrived and they chased the Spanish army all the way back to Spain.

In the town of Sterkdam there was a huge celebration! A massive bonfire was lit and the people of Sterkdam had a feast in the middle of the streets. Everyone ate and ate until they could eat no more.

And as for Tyl, that skinny thief ate so much that never again would he be able to slip through the bars of a prison cell window.

# 8: Captain Jack and the Bird

## (Carribean)

Once upon a time there lived a pirate called Captain Jack. This was Captain Jack Sparrow's cousin. He was most unlike Captain Jack Sparrow for this Captain Jack was mean, cruel, nasty and a bully. His name was Captain Jack Stinky.

Now Captain Jack Stinky lived on board a sailing ship with his pirate crew. But this crew lived in fear of Captain Jack because he always threatened to shoot them with his pistol or chop them to pieces with his cutlass if they didn't do as he said.

Captain Jack never shared his food or his grog and he especially never shared out his treasure.

One day, Captain Jack said, "I've got me an old treasure map. I'm gonna find this treasure and keep it all to meself. So NER-NER-NER-NER-NER-NEEEEEER!!!"

With that he sailed his ship to the treasure island and once there he climbed down the rope ladder and got into his rowing boat.

Then Captain Jack rowed his boat across the sea until he got to the treasure island.

He then followed his map as it took

him deep into the heart of the jungle until
he got to where the X marked the spot.
He then got out his spade and began to dig
for treasure. But as he was digging for
treasure, he suddenly heard a loud noise
that went . . .

     "NER-NER-NER-NER-NER-NEEEEER!!!"

Captain Jack looked all around and when he couldn't see anything, he carried on digging.

"NER-NER-NER-NER-NER-NEEEEER!!!" went the sound again.

Captain Jack looked up and there sat in a tree was a big, fat bluebird.

"NER-NER-NER-NER-NER-NEEEEER!!!" said the bluebird.

So Captain Jack took out his pistol and BOOM! he shot the bird and the bird fell out of the tree.

He then carried on digging, but soon stopped when he heard . . .
"NER-NER-NER-NER-NER-NEEEEER!!!"

"Yar!" he shouted. "It's that bird

again!"

Captain Jack went over to the bird and with his cutlass went CHOP! CHOP! CHOP! CHOP! CHOP! CHOP! and chopped the bird into a hundred pieces.

Next, he went back to the hole and began digging once more. At that moment he heard a THUD! as he had reached the treasure chest.

He pulled out the treasure chest, opened it up and there inside were thousands of golden coins!

Captain Jack smiled to himself. But as he was smiling he suddenly heard that noise again!

"NER-NER-NER-NER-NER-NEEEEER!!!"

"Yar!!!" he screamed. "It's that bird again!!!"

So Captain Jack went over to the bird, scooped up the hundred pieces of bird and put them into the hole he had just dug. He then used his spade to fill in the hole and wiped the sweat from his brow.

But as he was wiping the sweat from his brow, he suddenly heard another noise, a sort of muffled noise coming from underground. A noise that went . . .

"NER-NER-NER-NER-NER-NEEEEER.

"YAR!!!" he bellowed. "IT'S THAT
BIRD AGAIN!!!"

Captain Jack used his spade to dig up
the hundred bits off bird, tipped the
treasure onto the ground and put all one
hundred bits of bird into the treasure
chest. Next he closed the lid and locked the
padlock.

But there were one thousand golden
coins all over the floor. How could he get all
that back to his ship?

Well, he took two handfuls of treasure
and stuffed it into his pockets. When his
pockets were full he stuffed the treasure
down his shirt. When his shirt was filled he

then stuffed the treasure down his socks. And when his socks were filled, he stuffed the treasure down his pants.

But as Captain Jack stuffed the treasure down his pants, he suddenly heard that noise again, a sort of muffled noise coming from inside the treasure chest.

A noise that went . . .
"NER-NER-NER-NER-NER-NEEEEER!!!"

"YAR!!!" he bellowed. "IT'S THAT BIRD AGAIN!!!"

So Captain Jack heaved and dragged and pulled that treasure chest down to the beach and threw it out to sea.

Now with all that heaving and all that dragging and all that pulling, Captain Jack was exhausted, so he lay down on the sandy beach and fell fast asleep.

Meanwhile, that treasure chest went floating across the sea until it got to Captain Jack's sailing boat.

When the pirate crew on board the ship saw the treasure chest, they said, "Yar! Look! Treasure! And Captain Jack isn't here to take it from us, let's get it on board quickly!"

The pirates pulled the treasure chest up and on board the ship. They opened the treasure chest and out flew one hundred tiny, little bluebirds who covered the whole of the ship!

Some of them stood on the crow's nest, some of them stood on the poop deck,

some of then stood on the quarter deck, some of them stood on the bowsprit; they covered the whole of the ship!

Back on the treasure island, Captain Jack had woken up. He climbed into his rowing boat and rowed across the sea until he got to his sailing ship.

He dragged himself up the rope ladder and stood on the ship. Suddenly, Captain Jack saw one hundred tiny, little pairs of eyes all staring at him and one hundred tiny, little voices all shouted out, at the top of their voices . . .

"NER-NER-NER-NER-NER-NEEEEER!!!"

"YAR!!!" he screeched. "I CAN'T TAKE IT ANYMORE!!!"

With that Captain Jack leapt over board and landed in the water.

But with all that treasure in his pockets and down his shirt and in his socks and down his pants, he sank to bottom of the sea where he couldn't bully anyone ever again.

Those hundred blue birds all flew back

to the island that they came from.

And those pirates on board the sailing ship, without their horrid captain, all lived happily ever after.

*Also available in the Reluctant Reader Series*

PUBLISHING